The Comet of Doom

ren Wallace

ed by Helen Flook

Black • London

DRAWN

To Ivor, with love

First published 2009 by
A & C Black Publishers Ltd
36 Soho Square, London, W1D 3QY

www.acblack.com

ISBN 978-1-4081-1498-8

A CIP catalogue for this book is available from the British Library.

Printed and bound in Great
by CPI Cox & Wyman, Readir

Prologue

My name is Chantico and I am
an Aztec. My city, Tenochtitlan,
is the most beautiful place
under the sky. My ancestors
built it on an island in the
middle of a lake. Now there
are temples and palaces and
thousands of painted houses.
Each one has a garden full
of sweet-smelling flowers
and shady green trees.

When I look down from my secret place on the mountainside, I can see canals crisscrossing the city like blue ribbons and the tiny shapes of people paddling in their canoes.

I come here to write about Tenochtitlan in the word pictures of my language. My uncle, Ahcambal, who is soothsayer to our great king Moctezuma, gave me this special paper, which folds up like a map. He said it would last for ever, just like our wonderful city.

How was I to know my uncle would be wrong?

Chapter One

In some ways I live the same kind of life as any other Aztec boy of my class. My father, Tenoch, is a great warrior. He can throw his spear faster and further than anyone I know. But *I've* never wanted to be a warrior. I hated the wooden sword and shield my mother gave me to play with. I almost preferred the toy loom and apron that belonged to my sister, Tayanna. Well, *almost*. Being a girl isn't much fun unless you happen to like cooking, cleaning and embroidery.

As far as my father was concerned, there was nothing more glorious than being a warrior and dedicating your life to the service of our king. He was very proud that he had captured hundreds of prisoners, who had all been sacrificed to the god of war so the king would be successful in battle.

"How will *you* serve our Lord Moctezuma, Chantico?" he asked me, when I was still very young.

"I will be a soothsayer like Uncle Ahcambal, Father," I replied.

"What do *you* know about being a soothsayer?" my father demanded.

"I know what is going to happen before it happens," I said. "My uncle says I have the gift of second sight."

"What nonsense," my father snorted.

But it was true. It's something I've had ever since I was little. I would tell my mother that we were going to eat seaweed biscuits before she had even decided to cook them. Or to plant her corn seedlings because I knew it was going to rain. Sometimes I would see something in a dream before it actually happened. It was like looking into the future.

"Really, little know-all," my mother would say. "You must learn to keep your lucky guesses to yourself."

"He's nothing but a loud mouth," my father would add in a sour voice.

But something must have made them change their minds, because one day I was sent to study with my uncle. With him, I learnt how to paint word pictures, which is how we write down the ways of our people.

"You must draw lots of footprints – to show how far our ancestors walked to find the right place to build Tenochtitlan," my uncle would tell me, taking the brush from my hand. "And this shape, like a tiny puff of wind, shows when a man is speaking."

My older sister Tayanna never talked about my gift. She was too smart for that. She knew I wasn't lying and she never called me names.

In fact, Tayanna was the smartest girl I'd ever met. Not only could she remember all the legends Uncle Ahcambal taught me, she was brilliant at embroidery. She could make a word picture with a needle and thread almost as fast as I could paint one.

Now, here we were, sitting in our house by the canal, having one of our normal family conversations. As usual, my father was in a sulky mood because I wasn't a warrior like him, and my mother was making the pancakes we call *tortillas* and trying to keep the peace.

"If I was a warrior, I'd want to be like you, Father," said Tayanna sweetly, pretending not to notice the scowl on his face. "You are the best spear thrower in the city."

"You are very clever, for a girl," said my father in a self-mportant voice. He always liked being flattered. "Perhaps you should help your brother with his lessons."

My mother held out a plateful of *tortillas*. "How many would you like, Tayanna?"

The words were out of my mouth before I could stop them. "Three," I shouted. "She wants three!"

Then I burst out laughing because I could tell from the look on my sister's face that I was right.

"Chantico!" bellowed my father. "Where are your manners?"

I knew he was going to cuff me around the ears, so I ran into the street as fast as I could.

"Where are you going in such a hurry?"

It was my friend, Pochotl.

"I'm running away from my father's bad temper." I replied, looking over my shoulder.

"Do you want to come fishing?" asked Pochotl.

It was perfect timing.

"Yes! I'd *love* to come fishing!"

Pochotl grinned and held up his basket. "How many fish will we catch, little know-all?"

I closed my eyes and saw seven silver fish. "Four for me and three for you," I replied.

Pochotl smiled. Last week I had dreamed that King Moctezuma wanted to eat a dish of rabbit stewed in chilli and chocolate on his birthday. Pochotl had told his father, Maxtl, who was head of the royal kitchen, about my dream. And, sure enough, the king had been so delighted with his stew that he gave Maxtl a tiny rabbit carved out of gold.

Now Pochotl believes me when I say I have the gift of second sight.

"Three fish sounds good," said Pochotl. "By the way, my father says he owes you a favour."

I laughed. When would *I* ever need a favour from the head of the royal kitchen?

We ran along the edge of a canal, past men in canoes carrying melons and cooking pots and cages of chickens. I loved the way everyone called out greetings to each other as they paddled across the city.

Pochotl's canoe had two painted eyes to watch out for the water goddess.

We climbed in and he untied the twine that tied it to the wooden posts. I picked up the long pole that lay on the bottom and pushed us gently into the water.

Pochotl didn't go to the same school as me. He was training to be a carpenter. It was a friendship that suited us both. Pochotl showed me how to build wooden boxes to keep my word pictures dry. And I told him the stories my uncle Ahcambal taught me.

As we floated silently in the reeds by the lake shore, we found ourselves staring at the towering stone walls of the temples in the middle of the city. Even though they were miles away, they were so huge we could see the yellow stone sparkling in the sun.

Once, Uncle Ahcambal had taken me to the courtyard of the temples to see prisoners being sacrificed on the high altar. Hundreds of men stood silently on the steps with their heads bowed. My own father had probably captured some of them.

Everyone believed it was an honour for a captive to be sacrificed, but the thought of a sharp knife slicing into my chest had made me flinch, and I worried that Uncle Ahcambal might think I was a coward.

"Tell me a story," said Pochotl, as he let out his fishing line.

I looked across at the temple that was dedicated to the Feathered Serpent, the god that created our world. It was one of the tallest temples in the courtyard.

"One day, legend says that the Feathered Serpent will come down from the sky and destroy everything," I began. Then I stopped because Pochotl was shouting with laughter.

"I asked for a *story*," he cried. "Not a *joke*!"

But as he laughed, the air turned cold around us and I found myself shivering. Somehow, it felt like Pochotl was laughing at the Feathered Serpent himself, which was a dangerous thing to do. No matter how small the insult, gods always take revenge.

Chapter Two

My mother was delighted with my fish because Uncle Ahcambal was coming to supper.

"Put a cloth on the table, Tayanna," she said as she stirred some beans and added the hot, peppery sauce we call *tamale* to the pot. "Your uncle likes his food to be laid out nicely, like it is at the palace."

Tayanna put down the cactus needle she was using to embroider a shirt and spread a white cotton cloth over the low wooden table. She had made the cloth herself and embroidered the edges with red and yellow fruit and vegetables.

My mother nodded approvingly. "You, Chantico," she said. "Put water and cups on the table and a jug of *pulque* for your uncle."

Pulque was a strong drink made from cactus juice. Only older men were allowed to drink it because too much made you say silly things and fall over. The king preferred chocolate flavoured with spices. Perhaps he had heard too many old men talking nonsense. I had never tasted *pulque*, but I had already decided that when *I* grew up, I would only drink chocolate, like the king.

"Shall I put out a jug for Father?" I asked, reaching up to the shelf where we kept our pottery.

My mother shook her head. "A war of flowers has been demanded by the priests. He has gone off to fight."

I put one jug on the table. If there were no *real* wars going on and no captives being taken, the priests arranged *pretend* battles between warriors called "wars of flowers". The warriors who lost were sacrificed to keep the gods satisfied. So far, my father had always been a winner.

My mother looked out onto the street. The sun had almost gone from the sky and there was still no sign of Uncle Ahcambal. She pointed to the plate of *tortillas*. "Eat these to keep your stomachs quiet," she said, putting on her cloak. "I will send word to your uncle. He must have forgotten my invitation."

As soon as Mother had left, Tayanna spread the *tortillas* with chilli paste and handed one to me. "Tell me about the Feathered Serpent," she said.

I stared at her. "Why do you ask about him?" I said.

Tayanna shrugged. "His name just popped into my head," she replied. "I was thinking about all the prisoners we sacrifice, then I remembered that you told me the Feathered Serpent was not as hungry for blood as the other gods."

I smiled shakily. Sometimes Tayanna has a way of reading my mind. She wanted to hear the same story I had started to tell Pochotl.

"The Feathered Serpent made our world," I said. I looked down at my hands and saw they were trembling. "But legend says that one day he will come down from the sky and destroy everything."

Tayanna's eyes widened. "Surely he won't destroy his own people?"

"I don't know," I replied. "No one knows."

A strange noise filled the night. Our little dog, Zolin, threw back his head and began to howl as if he was about to die. I realised then that the noise was the sound of every dog in the city howling at the same time.

My mother rushed into the room. "Go to your sleeping mats," she ordered. "The priests have called this night unlucky." She grabbed Zolin and threw him outside.

"Please, Mother," I cried. "Let Zolin stay inside."

"Quiet, little know-all!" she shouted at me. "Do what you're told for once!"

Chapter Three

When I woke up, I was standing with Zolin in front of the royal palace. My heart was pounding. I had sleepwalked half a mile from our house!

It was still dark, but the sky was bright with stars and the lake shone silver in the moonlight. As I stared up at the palace, I saw a man by a window in a brightly lit room. As he turned, gold ornaments flashed in his ears and green feathers glimmered on his cloak. I almost cried out. Only one person wore a cloak of green feathers... Our great king, Moctezuma!

I threw myself onto the ground. To see his face was an act punishable by death.

The air filled with a loud, ragged whistling. I looked up and saw a ball of flames racing in a great arc across the sky.

As I stared, it turned into a fiery monster with a gigantic head and a long, streaming tail. A shower of burning embers, like sparks from a god's fire, fell away from the tail and tumbled towards the earth.

I heard a cry from the window. It was the voice of King Moctezuma!

＊

I reached my house before the sun had climbed into the sky, then I lay down on my mat in the shadowy room where Tayanna was still asleep. I closed my eyes and dreamed the strangest dream.

The Feathered Serpent appeared in front of me. His head was so huge, it blotted out the sun. When he opened his fanged mouth, I saw an ocean inside it.

Floating mountains moved over the water, coming closer and closer to our land. I saw rowing boats appear from inside the mountains. Strange men with white skin and black hair on their faces pulled at the oars. Some of them carried sticks that spat out fire.

One man stood in front of the rest. He held his hand high and pointed towards the heart of our land. Somehow,

I knew that this man was the Feathered Serpent in disguise and that he had come to destroy us.

As I stared, the Feathered Serpent threw back his head and spat thousands of my people into the air. As they hit the ground, their bodies smashed into pieces like pottery dolls.

I woke to the sound of wailing in the street. I rushed downstairs. My mother was slumped on the floor, crying. Beside her, Tayanna was trying to start a fire.

"What's happened?" I cried. "Why didn't you wake me?"

"I tried," replied Tayanna. "But you wouldn't open your eyes." She knelt forward and blew a long steady breath into a pile of wood shavings. A tiny flame flickered and caught light.

"Last night, a ball of fire ripped open the sky," sobbed my mother. "No one knows what it means. Uncle Ahcambal is with the king now."

The words were out of my mouth before I could stop them. "I know what it means," I blurted. "I had a —"

My mother jerked her head up and her eyes blazed with fury. "Shut your mouth," she yelled at me. "How could you, a silly boy, know about such a thing?" She whacked a griddle against the flat stones around the fire and broke it. "The king has already killed ten soothsayers who had no answers."

My father walked into the room. His face was grim. "I have just heard that Ahcambal is to be executed," he said to my mother in a low voice. "He couldn't tell the king the meaning of the ball of fire, either."

My mother pulled her apron over her head and howled. My uncle Ahcambal was her only brother.

"Father!" I cried. "I –"

My father held up his hand for silence and knelt beside my mother. "Don't worry," he told her. "I have taken so many captives, I will ask the king to free Ahcambal as a favour to me."

As soon as he had left, my mother put on her cloak. "I am going to pray," she said in a choked voice. "There is nothing else I can do."

When we were alone, I told Tayanna about my dream. I looked her straight in the eyes. "I *know* I am right," I said. "I *know* it will happen."

"But who will believe you?" replied my sister. "He is a silly boy. A know-all. That's what they'll say."

"If only I could tell the king about my dream and my gift," I said. "Then I would let him know that Ahcambal is my teacher." I shuddered. "Our Lord Moctezuma is the wisest man under the sun. Surely he would summon our uncle to ask if I am telling the truth."

Tayanna picked up her embroidery. "That may be," she said. "But the king would never agree to see you. We must put our hope in Father instead."

I found myself staring at the embroidered cloth in Tayanna's hands. Suddenly, I had an idea!

I knew from Pochotl that each day the king had a new tablecloth laid for his midday meal. What if Tayanna embroidered everything we wanted to tell the king in word pictures on the edge of a tablecloth? Pochotl's father said he owed me a favour. If he could make sure Tayanna's cloth was on the royal table, there was a chance King Moctezuma would read my story and ask to see Uncle Ahcambal for an explanation. The problem was I needed to be there, too, just in case things went wrong.

My father rushed into the room. "Where is your mother?" he shouted. He was sweating and out of breath. He must have run all the way back from the palace.

"She went to pray for Uncle Ahcambal," I replied. I didn't dare ask him if the king had refused his favour. From the black look on his face, it was obvious.

"Ahcambal is to be executed after the sinking of two suns," said my father, grimly. "I'll go and tell your mother myself." He walked out of the door and left us alone.

Tayanna put down her cloth and burst into tears.

"Don't cry," I said, sitting down beside her.

Tayanna's face was blotchy and tear-stained. "You heard Father," she sobbed. "The king has spoken and there's nothing we can do."

I wiped her wet cheek with my hand. "Listen, sister," I said. "I've got a plan."

Chapter Four

Tayanna said nothing as I told her my idea. When I had finished, she still said nothing. I threw my hands in the air. "Well, can you think of anything better?"

Tayanna stood up and unhooked her basket from the wall. "I will need threads of different colours and a length of the finest cloth," she said, briskly. "Do you have enough paper and paints?"

I stared at her. "So you like my plan?"

Tayanna laughed. "It's *brilliant*, you clever little know-all," she cried. "I'll collect some eggs for bartering, then we must get to the market right away."

An hour later, we stood in the middle of the market square at the north end of the city. It was like being inside the biggest beehive on earth. Thousands of people were shouting and haggling at the same time.

In front of me, a man was carrying an enormous sack of chilli peppers on his back. Onions and squashes hung down on strings from a band around his head. As he made his way through the crowd, selling his vegetables, he roared like a bull. Then we passed a medicine woman pulling vipers out of a basket. Their blood was known to give extra strength in battle. Around her, five little boys were doing somersaults and cartwheels for pieces of broken *tortilla*.

Tayanna grabbed my arm and led me quickly through the crowd to a row of stalls on the eastern side of the square. Here there were rolls of cloth and mounds of different-coloured threads piled high on the stony ground.

Tayanna knew exactly what she wanted and bought it in exchange for her six eggs.

"Are you sure you have enough paper?" she shouted above the yells of the crowd.

I nodded. I had already thought out some of the word pictures I was going to paint. Now I wanted to go home and get started. There was no time to lose.

※

Two days later, before dawn, Tayanna put the finished tablecloth in my hands. She was so tired, she was cross-eyed, and the ends of her fingers were red with tiny pricks from the cactus needle. "Good luck," she said. Then she rolled herself in a blanket and fell asleep by the fire.

I spread the cloth out by the fire and pretended I was the king seeing it for the first time. Tayanna had done a brilliant job. The first picture showed how Uncle Ahcambal was part of my family and how he had taught me the legend of the Feathered Serpent. Then I saw the fiery ball and my dream, just as I had explained them to Tayanna. When you looked at one picture, you wanted to read them all.

I quickly folded up the cloth and ran out into the busy street. While Tayanna had been embroidering her pictures, I had been to visit Pochotl's father.

At first Maxtl had refused to help. Royal handmaidens put the cloth on the king's table and it was impossible to smuggle me into the dining room.

"You cannot pretend to be a servant," he said. "And King Moctezuma's singers have the finest voices in the city. What if the king asks you to sing? He will know you are a fake and kill us both."

So I sang him a song. Luckily, I have a beautiful voice.

Maxtl closed his eyes and said nothing. It was as if he was praying to the gods for advice. "I will help you," he said at last.

✻

Now, as I reached the servants' quarters at

the palace, I was shaking like a leaf.

"You must hurry, Chantico," said Maxtl. "Preparations for the king's meal have already begun."

"But the sun is barely in the sky," I replied. "I thought the king ate his lunch at midday."

"The priests have consulted new omens," replied Maxtl. "Your uncle is to be killed at noon. The king will eat early." He looked down at the folded cloth in my hands. "What is this?"

"The tablecloth my sister made."

Maxtl frowned. "There is already a fresh cloth on the king's table."

My stomach turned over. "I told you!" I cried. "The king must see my pictures and learn my story. It's my uncle's only hope!"

Maxtl looked into my eyes. Whatever he saw there made him change his mind.

"Don't worry, little know-all," he said and took the tablecloth from my hands.

Maxtl led me down a long corridor that seemed to go on for miles. The sound of my bare feet slapping down on the polished stone floors echoed around us. I was so nervous I could barely look at the brightly painted walls or the beautifully carved sculptures that stood in every corner.

I made myself breathe slowly. It was too late to turn back now.

Maxtl opened a door and showed me into a room with an enormous bath of steaming hot water set into the floor. "Wash yourself here," he said. "A servant will come to dress you shortly."

Five minutes later, my body shone with oil and my hair was smoothed back. I wore a new scarlet loincloth and a necklace of shells hung around my neck.

As the servant left, a man dressed in the cloak of the king's house guard appeared. "The dining room is prepared," he said. "You must join the others and wait." He paused and fixed me with his coal-black eyes. "One thing, singer. The king is in a dark mood. Should you perform, be sure to choose a sad song."

I bowed and followed him into a long room filled with flowers. Water from a fish-shaped fountain sprayed into the air and made a soothing, pattering sound as it fell. I took my place by a palm tree planted into the ground. Two white-faced monkeys watched me curiously from the spiky leaves and a parrot fluttered over my head.

There was something magical about the room. It was like walking into a hidden clearing in the jungle. All the walls were painted pale green and inlaid with a pattern of turquoise and orange tiles. Tapestries embroidered with birds and butterflies hung from the ceiling, and the floor was covered with rugs of all colours.

At the far end of the room, I could see a gold screen in front of the throne. My hands went cold and clammy. The screen must be there so the king could eat from

his table without being watched. But then how would I tell if he had noticed my pictures? I had to get nearer to the throne.

I waited for what seemed like ages. Then a sense of fear and excitement rippled through the room. Two men on either side of the throne stepped forward and began to wave fans made of feathers. Servants appeared, walking silently and carrying trays and tables and cushions.

I followed them and got as close as possible to one side of the screen. Then everyone fell to their knees and put their faces on the floor, and I did the same.

There was the sound of cloaks rustling and sandals lightly hitting the ground. Furniture scraped on tiles. Someone clapped their hands and we all sat up. I saw a long line of servants standing along the wall, holding dishes of food. One at a time, they walked up to the gold screen and held out their dish. Each time, they went quickly away. It was clear the king wasn't hungry.

I tried to see whether Tayanna's cloth was on the table, but it was impossible.

Someone hissed in my ear. "You, new face! Sing a song!"

I was pushed forwards and, even though my eyes were fixed on the ground, I knew I was standing very near to the throne.

I began to sing the saddest song I could remember. It was about a day when morning didn't come because the sun had lost its way during the night. As I sang, I turned my head a fraction and suddenly saw the king looking down at my tablecloth. He was reading my story!

I was so scared, my voice dried up completely ... and I slumped to the floor.

Chapter Five

A guard grabbed me by the neck and hissed in my ear. "You are no singer." A knife blade dug into my back. "Traitors will be killed."

"Please!" I croaked. "I am not a traitor. My uncle is soothsayer to the king."

"Only a traitor would come before the king unannounced," snarled the voice. The blade dug deeper.

I had nothing to lose. "Great Lord Moctezuma," I cried. "My name is Chantico!"

You could have heard a snake slither across the floor. I closed my eyes and waited for the pain of the knife.

Instead, I heard a voice shouting. "Bring me the soothsayer, Ahcambal!"

It seemed as if time stood still. Then my head was pulled back even further and I found myself looking at my uncle.

"Is this boy your nephew?" demanded the guard.

Uncle Ahcambal's face was like chalk. "Yes," he replied. "But I do not know why he is here."

"Speak, boy," ordered the guard.

I could barely breathe. My plan had worked! Now I had the chance to tell my story to the king. The problem was I couldn't say a word, because my head was pulled back so far.

"Fool!" growled another voice. "How can he speak if you break his neck?"

Every hair on my body stood on end. It was King Moctezuma!

The man let go of me and, trying not to stumble on my words, I told Uncle Ahcambal everything that had happened since I had seen the fiery ball. Just as the king had read in my word pictures.

There was the sound of a stave hitting the floor. "Approach, Ahcambal!" ordered Moctezuma's voice.

Uncle Ahcambal threw himself full length on the floor and dragged himself towards the throne.

"Do you believe your nephew?"

My uncle hesitated and I thought I was going to be sick. "Yes, Great One," he said at last. "Chantico has the gift."

"Why didn't you tell me about him?" asked the king in a dangerous voice. "It is your duty to make such things known."

Now I knew why my uncle had hesitated. His life depended on his reply.

"Chantico is still young, Great One," replied my uncle. "I have much more to teach him. A child who can read the future can also be understood in the wrong way."

"What is this wrong way?" asked the king. It was obvious he still hadn't decided what he was going to do with either of us.

"The boy is often called a know-all by his elders," said Uncle Ahcambal, nervously. "It is said against his youth, not the interpretations of his visions."

There was a silence. My heart was beating so loud, I was sure the king could hear it. What he said next would mean life or death for all my family.

"The things this boy has told us are serious and need much discussion." Moctezuma banged his stave again.

"I shall have this know-all in my service. Approach, Chantico!"

I couldn't move. Then a foot prodded me and I shuffled up on my stomach beside my uncle.

"You will live in the palace," said the king. "And in honour of your sister's skill and trustworthiness, she will join you." He paused. "You are pardoned, Ahcambal. You have done your duty.

I see now that the right way forward was not clear at the beginning."

I rolled my eyes upwards and saw the kings' gold sandals a hand's width from my face. He stood and I heard the swish of his feathered cloak as he walked away.

Uncle Ahcambal pulled me up and held me tightly to his chest. "Chantico!" he cried. "I owe you and Tayanna my life. Come! We will tell your parents."

Word travels faster than an eagle flies in our city. By the time we got home, my mother was dressed in her finest clothes and was wailing with joy.

"My son, the king's soothsayer! My daughter, the king's embroiderer! My brother, the wisest of men!" And, for the first time in my life, my father told me he was proud that I was his son.

"I'm glad your plan worked," said Tayanna, almost shyly when the grown-ups went outside.

I wanted to say that nothing would have worked without the tablecloth she had embroidered, but before I could speak, one of the king's guards marched into the room.

"The king bids you to the palace," he said. "Your sister is to join you when the sun has gone from the sky." He held out a woven bag. "This is for you."

My hands shook as I looked in the bag. Inside was a white loincloth and a blue cloak made of heavy cotton, decorated with red and yellow beads. As I took out the cloak, a small box tumbled to the floor. A green feather was fixed to its lid and it was tied with a piece of purple thread.

"It's a present from King Moctezuma,"

said Tayanna. "Those are his colours."

I picked up the box, but I could barely bring myself to touch the green feather. It was as if I was touching the king himself.

As I untied the thread and eased open the lid, Tayanna's eyes sparkled.

Inside was a clasp for the cloak in the shape of two hummingbirds with their beaks touching. The gold birds were set with turquoise and jade stones and their wings were outlined in silver. It was the most beautiful clasp I had ever seen.

I put the cloak around my shoulders and remembered my father's question when I was a little boy. *And how will you serve our Lord Moctezuma, Chantico? My heart surged as I heard my reply. I will be a soothsayer like Uncle Ahcambal.*

And so it had happened as I foretold.

I stepped proudly onto the street and set off towards the palace.

Epilogue

My name is Chantico and I am an Aztec. Ten years have passed since I first became soothsayer to King Moctezuma and now I am a man.

Once, my city, Tenochtitlan, was the most beautiful place under the sky. Now there are only shattered walls and broken roofs where temples and palaces once stood. Our king is dead and thousands of my people have been killed. The ones that are left hunt like starving dogs among the smoking ruins.

I have written my story in the word pictures of our language.

You see, I was right about the white man with black hair. Three years ago, he arrived with others who carried sticks that spat out fire. He killed our king and destroyed our land and our people.

But I was wrong, too. The white man wasn't the Feathered Serpent in disguise. His name was Hernán Cortés, and he was evil and greedy. He came from a land called Spain and he wanted to steal our gold and turn our people into slaves.

As I finish the last picture and put it on a stone to dry, Tayanna comes up behind me. She looks much older and her eyes are dull. All our family are dead because of Hernán Cortés. Even my father, who believed he would never die in battle, was killed by a stick that spat out fire.

You might say we are lucky to be alive. Sometimes, I don't think so.

"Why are you still painting word pictures?" Tayanna asks me. "What will you do with them?"

The paint is dry. I fold up the last piece of my special paper and put it on a pile with the others. "I am going to wrap them up and bury them in a cave."

Tayanna looks at me as if I am joking. "What on earth for?"

"Because one day, hundreds of years from now, someone will find them," I tell her, "and they will want to read the true story of our people."

This is something I have been thinking about for a long time and I know I am right.

Tayanna smiles. For the first time in weeks, I see a sparkle in her eyes. "Then I'm sure it will happen," she says. "You always were a clever little know-all!"